OFFICIAL
GUIDE

©LEVEL-5/YWP. Produced by Scholastic Inc.
under license from LEVEL-5.

Published by Scholastic Inc., *Publishers since 1920.* SCHOLASTIC and associated
logos are trademarks and/or registered trademarks of Scholastic Inc.

The publisher does not have any control over and does not assume any responsibility
for author or third-party websites or their content.

No part of this publication may be reproduced, stored in a retrieval system, or transmitted
in any form or by any means, electronic, mechanical, photocopying,
recording, or otherwise, without written permission of the publisher.
For information regarding permission, write to Scholastic Inc., Attention:
Permissions Department, 557 Broadway, New York, NY 10012.

This book is a work of fiction. Names, characters, places, and incidents are either the product of
the author's imagination or are used fictitiously, and any resemblance to actual persons, living
or dead, business establishments, events, or locales is entirely coincidental.

ISBN 978-1-338-05442-2

10 9 8 7 6 5 4 3 2 1   16 17 18 19 20

Printed in the U.S.A.   40

First printing 2016

OFFICIAL GUIDE

By Meredith Rusu

SCHOLASTIC INC.

Introduction

Main Characters

Rules of the Yo-kai World

Meet the Yo-kai

Other Characters

Conclusion

WELCOME **TO THE** WORLD OF YO-KAI!

Mysterious things happen every day. Little things that annoy you in a BIG way. Like when you forget someone's name, accidentally eat too much fast food, or have to go to the bathroom at the *worst* possible time.

Everyone thinks these daily annoyances are just part of life. But what if that's not the whole story? What if something *supernatural* is to blame?

In the city of Springdale, that's exactly what's going on! Mischievous beings called Yo-kai are causing mayhem all around town, making people do and say things they don't mean to. The Yo-kai float through streets and roam school halls, and no one can see them!

Sometimes the Yo-kai are playful. Other times they're devious. But one thing is for certain—when there's a Yo-kai around, something funky is about to go down!

Welcome to the World of Yo-kai!

Fifth-grader Nate Adams isn't like everyone else. He thought annoying things like forgetting to study for a big test or letting out a stinky fart in class were just bad luck. But all that changed the day a Yo-kai named Whisper gave Nate the Yo-kai Watch. Using the watch, Nate can see the Yo-kai all around Springdale. And now it's up to him to help them solve their problems and befriend them! (Or at least keep them from making him toot in class.) Since that day, Nate's life has never been the same . . .

What Are Yo-kai?

Yo-kai are strange, supernatural beings who cause life's everyday annoyances. No one can see or hear them, but when someone does something he or she doesn't mean to, there's a good chance a Yo-kai is to blame.

Each Yo-kai has a different backstory and causes people to do different things. Some Yo-kai are the embodiments of people, animals, or even household objects who have unfinished business in the living world. Other Yo-kai just, well, *are*.

Yo-kai don't want to hurt people . . . exactly. But they love playing pranks and making weird stuff happen. Every time someone is possessed, or "inspirited" by a Yo-kai, he or she is subjected to that Yo-kai's power. Yo-kai can keep people awake all night, make them brag or spill secrets, or even convince you to spend all your allowance on useless stuff. Talk about annoying!

Nate Adams

Nate Adams used to be just an ordinary fifth grader like any other. He worried about tests, cleaning his room, and fitting in at school.

But there was one thing Nate didn't want: for his friends to think he was *average*. Nothing is worse than being average. Average is basically another word for *boring*.

So one fateful day, while Nate and his friends were searching for cool bugs, Nate decided to go deeper into the woods than any of the other kids. He wanted to find the biggest, most impressive bug ever. That was where he discovered something . . . strange. Something that would change his life forever.

All About Nate

Name: Nathan (Nate) Adams
Grade: Five
Friends: Bear, Eddie, Katie
School: Springdale Elementary
Quote: "Yo-kai Medal, do your thing!"

Yo-kai Are Real!

Deep in the forest, Nate stumbled upon an ancient stone capsule machine. Before he knew what he was doing, Nate inserted a coin, opened the capsule that popped out, and *whoosh*! A strange being named Whisper appeared!

Whisper explained that he was a *Yo-kai*: A fantastical being who had been trapped in the capsule machine for 190 years. Because Nate had set him free, Whisper insisted he was forever in the boy's debt. Nate was totally uninterested— he had better things to do. But Whisper wouldn't take no for an answer—and so their unlikely friendship began.

Whisper's Yo-kai Pad

Each time Nate and Whisper encounter a Yo-kai, Whisper reads information about it from his handy-dandy Yo-kai Pad. It's basically a digital encyclopedia for the supernatural world. Nate asked how Whisper got it. Whisper told him to not worry about the details.

Self-proclaimed butler Yo-kai →

Loud-mouthed, smart-mouthed, big-mouthed: Whisper is all these things and so much more. This high-spirited being is a self-proclaimed butler Yo-kai.

Whisper is Nate's guide to the Yo-kai world and helps him navigate through all the sticky, tricky, and downright icky Yo-kai experiences they face each day. For the most part, Whisper tries to help. But he has a habit of pretending to know more than he does and conveniently forgetting to tell Nate important information.

All About Whisper

Tribe: ???

Abilities: Guide; being annoying

Backstory: Locked in a capsule machine 190 years ago by monks who deemed him a menace to society. Who knew monks had such a sense of humor?

Quote: "What is up, my corporeal friend?"

whisper

The Yo-kai Watch

Soon after meeting, Whisper gave Nate the mysterious Yo-kai Watch. And it sure isn't your granddaddy's old-fashioned timepiece! The Yo-kai Watch allows Nate to see the Yo-kai creating mischief around town so he can stop them.

But the watch came with a catch—Nate can never take it off. Plus, now he can see Yo-kai everywhere!

Nate isn't a hero, but he's the only one who can summon Yo-kai to take care of the situation. And with the Yo-kai turning his life upside down, he doesn't really have a choice but to use the watch.

Pressing the button on the side of the Yo-kai Watch causes it to light up, illuminating any Yo-kai hiding nearby.

Nate's Top Ten Priorities
Before and After Discovering Yo-kai

BYK (Before Yo-kai)

1) Fitting in
2) Impressing his friends
3) Showing Katie he isn't just average
4) Getting good grades
5) Fitting in
6) Not embarrassing himself in school
7) Keeping his room clean
8) Fitting in
9) Saving his allowance to buy cool stuff
10) Did we mention fitting in?

AYK (After Yo-kai)

1) Becoming friends with the Yo-kai
2) Stopping Yo-kai from ruining his life
3) Stopping Yo-kai from messing with his friends
4) Stopping Yo-kai from making his parents argue
5) Stopping Yo-kai from making him forget things
6) Stopping Yo-kai from making him have to go to the bathroom
7) Stopping Yo-kai from making his *friends* have to go to the bathroom
8) Stopping Yo-kai from making him say "no way" to cool stuff
9) Stopping Yo-kai from getting him in trouble with teachers, parents, friends, and pretty much everyone else
10) Fitting in (as much as a boy who can see invisible Yo-kai *can* fit in)

Main Characters

Katie Forester

Katie is super sweet. She's one of Nate's closest friends. But just because she has a big heart doesn't mean she's a pushover. Katie can hold her own in just about anything, whether it's playing sports or hunting for cool bugs with the guys. Nate has a huge crush on her. Unfortunately, she barely remembers he exists because he's so average! And the Yo-kai are constantly causing confusion between them.

Barnaby (Bear) Bernstein

Barnaby, or Bear, looks and talks tough. But underneath his gruff appearance, he's really a big softie. The Yo-kai have a habit of making Bear do awkward things, like bragging about how fast a runner he is (he isn't) or thinking he got a perfect score on a test (he didn't). Nate watches out for Bear, and even though Bear gives Nate a hard time (he doesn't), he has Nate's back when the chips are down.

Edward (Eddie) Archer

Eddie is the whiz kid of Nate's group—always ready to explain a homework problem or look up a cool fact on his smartphone. Even if Nate told Eddie about the Yo-kai, Eddie probably wouldn't believe him unless science could explain it. That makes it especially awkward when a Yo-kai causes Eddie to do something embarrassing, like act tough or make student-council promises he can't keep!

There are eight different Yo-kai tribes.

Some Yo-kai are happy, helpful, and just trying to mind their own business. Others are full-on, in-your-face-but-you-can't-see-them annoying! Each Yo-kai's personality determines which tribe he or she belongs to.

♥ Charming

Yo-kai in the Charming tribe are cute and endearing. Many of them just want attention and affection. Komajiro, Jibanyan, and Komasan belong to the Charming tribe.

Alarming, boom, boom! Walla, walla, dance, dance, Charming!

Brave

Brave Yo-kai are cool, courageous beings who excel at battling, especially physical combat. Blazion, B3-NK1, Sheen, and Shogunyan all belong to the Brave tribe.

Sumo shave! Flavo engrave! Flash team'a Brave!

Tough

> Gruff stuff!
> Rough bluff!
> Red ban, jacket stand,
> bling blang, Tough!

These Yo-kai are the toughest of mind and body. They can be extremely stubborn and bad-to-the-bone. But they also give some of the strongest defense in confrontation. Noway, Robonyan, Roughraff, and Fidgephant all belong to the Tough tribe.

Mysterious

> Boo-shiggy, boo-shiggy, boogie woogie! Cling-clang delirious, Mysterious!

The eccentric Yo-kai in the Mysterious tribe look strange and act even stranger. From spilling secrets to changing your television channels, there's no telling what they'll do. Tattletell, Tengu, Signibble, and Kyubi all belong to the Mysterious tribe.

Speedy artful!
Sing la-la-la!
Everywhere
Heartful!

Heartful

The Heartful tribe is home to some of the most helpful Yo-kai. They lift your spirits, have touching backstories, and can't help pouring their hearts out. Hungramps, Happierre, Enerfly, and Wiglin, Steppa, and Rhyth all belong to the Heartful tribe.

Eerie

There's no getting around it —Eerie Yo-kai are weird. From Manjimutt, who is half middle-aged man, half dog, to Cheeksqueek, whose face is literally a tush, Eerie Yo-kai give people the creeps! Other members of the Eerie tribe include Dismarelda and Rockabelly.

Lookie-lee, lookie-lee, flippidy-dee!
Lookie-lee, lookie-lee, bubba Eerie!

Shady

Members of the Shady tribe are the gloomiest Yo-kai of the bunch. They hang out in the shadows, inspiriting people to do the same—and to withdraw from their friends and family. Hidabat, Timidevil, Dimmy, and Tengloom all belong to Shady.

> Marvelous thee! Gusty, free banshee! Sing, sing Shady!

> Trippery! Glippery! Slimey-wimey do, Slippery!

Slippery

Super hard to get ahold of, the wiggly Yo-kai of the Slippery tribe do their own thing and go their own way. If a Slippery Yo-kai is messing with your life, good luck catching it. Venoct, Noko, Dragon Lord, and Cynake all belong to this tribe.

Legendary

In addition to the eight tribes, there are also the rarest of the rare Legendary Yo-kai. Not much is known about these Yo-kai—other than that if you collect enough Yo-kai Medals, they'll appear. Shogunyan is one of the Legendary Yo-kai we do know about.

Imaginary! Incendiary! Flip flap, squiggle boom, slim slam, Legendary!

Negotiation or Confrontation

When **Whisper** gave **Nate** the Yo-kai Watch, he explained that the only way to stop a Yo-kai is through negotiation or confrontation. Nate can either befriend a troublesome Yo-kai, or he can battle it. Luckily, Nate is not on his own. He has friends to help him!

Yo-kai Medals

Each Yo-kai possesses a medal that is the sign of their friendship. Once Nate befriends or defeats a Yo-kai, he gains its medal and, in turn, its trust. From that moment on, Nate can place the medal in the Yo-kai Watch to summon his friends for help.

Yo-kai Medal, do your thing!

The Yo-kai Medallium

Whisper also gave Nate the Yo-kai Medallium. This book keeps Nate's hard-earned medals safe and sound. It also keeps them all in one place, so Nate doesn't lose them (he really isn't the tidiest person in the world).

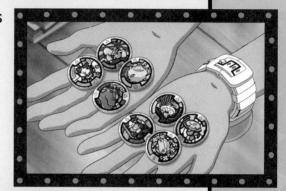

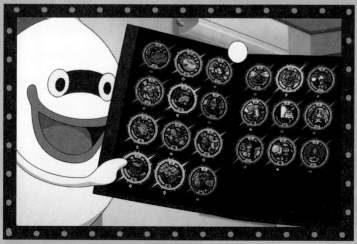

Meet the Yo-kai

Dismarelda is one gloomy Gus. She's a giant purple blob of moodiness that causes tension wherever she goes. People inspirited by Dismarelda suddenly feel sullen, depressed, or argumentative for no reason. Talk about a downer!

Dismarelda was the first Yo-kai Nate met after Whisper, and they didn't get off on the right foot. Dismarelda made Nate's parents argue over yogurt (yes, yogurt). Whisper explained that this was a very common phenomenon for a Yo-kai, called "arguing over nothing." If Nate didn't stop her, Dismarelda could make his parents argue forever!

All About Dismarelda

Tribe: Eerie
Ability: Causes depression, conflict, and discord
Married to: Happierre
Secret: Worries her husband doesn't love her
Catchphrase: "No filter"

Nate tried to negotiate by asking Dismarelda to leave. As it turned out, she herself was feeling down because she'd had an argument with her husband, Happierre. Nate explained even happy couples fight sometimes, and with a little convincing (and some help from Whisper), Dismarelda was able to see the light.

Can you feel the love? If so, there's a good chance Happierre is around. This Heartful Yo-kai emits warmth and joy, lightening the mood wherever he goes. He's married to Dismarelda, and the two cancel each other out, creating normalcy. One of Happierre's key tricks for keeping his Dis-baby happy is his alluring French laughter. *Awh-haw-haw!*

Just when Nate thought he wouldn't be able to convince Dismarelda to leave his parents alone, Whisper came to the rescue and called in Happierre. The cheery Yo-kai assured his Dis-baby that he still loved her, and they went on their merry way. As soon as they left, Nate's parents went back to being normal. And Nate had two new Yo-kai Medals to add to his collection!

All About Happierre

Tribe: Heartful
Ability: Makes people feel happy
Married to: Dismarelda
Motto: Ze French way is ze happy way.
Speaks with: A French accent

Happierre

Before he became a Yo-kai, Jibanyan used to be a pet cat owned by a girl named Amy. He loved his life as a cat! He would sleep in the bed, on the sofa, under the table—everything was perfect.

Then, one fateful day, poor Jibanyan was hit by a truck and turned into a Yo-kai.

Ever since then, Jibanyan has sworn vengeance upon all cars and trucks. He spends his days training at intersections, hoping that one day he can face Amy again.

Paws of Fury! Nya-nya-nya-nya-nya!

All About Jibanyan

Tribe: Charming

Ability: Inspirits people to walk into traffic

Special Attack: Paws of Fury

Loves: Chocobars and taking naps

Favorite Girl Band: Next HarMEOWny

Catchphrase: "I'm busy right *nyow*." / "What is it *nyow*, Nyate?"

At first, Nate thought he would have to battle Jibanyan in order to keep the little guy from causing car accidents. But after hearing Jibanyan's backstory, Nate realized that all the sad Yo-kai wanted was to be loved. He offered to be Jibanyan's friend, and even let Jibanyan move in with him so the Yo-kai wouldn't feel lonely. Jibanyan was overjoyed, and he's stuck to Nate like glue ever since!

Jibanyan's Sing-Along

I am a cat, and I like it like that!
I wash my butt in a Laundromat.
I am a cat, and I like it like that!
I tell half truths like a diplomat.

A Day in the Life of Jibanyan

8:00 a.m.: Wake up. Go back to sleep. It's too early *nyow*.

9:00 a.m.: Wake up for real. Eat chocobars.

11:30 a.m.: Hit the intersections. PAWS OF FURY!!

11:35 a.m.: Nap.

1:30 p.m.: Lunchtime. Chocobars . . .

2:00 p.m.: Put up new Next HarMEOWny posters in Nate's room.

2:30 p.m.: Get summoned by Nate for a Yo-kai battle. (Ugh, what is it *nyow*, Nyate?)

2:35 p.m.: *Nyo nyo nyo!* What IS that Yo-kai! I don't wanna battle!

2:45 p.m.: Leave the battling to Nate and Whisper. Nap.

5:00 p.m.: Rush hour. Those cars HAD IT COMIN'!

6:00 p.m.: Dinner. Choco-choco-choco-choco.

7:30 p.m.: Watch a tearjerker movie with Whisper. Yo-kai have all the feels, too.

10:00 p.m.: Bedtime. I'm a cat, and I like it like tha . . . ZZZZZZZZZZZZZZZZ.

Jibanyan

Shogunyan

Not much is known about this mysterious cat Yo-kai. He is a Legendary Yo-kai, meaning he only appears once Nate has collected enough Yo-kai Medals. Shogunyan says he is Jibanyan's ancestor, and he is extremely skilled with a samurai sword. Centuries may have passed, but don't mess with this kitty's dessert, or you might find yourself sliced in two!

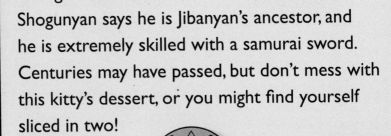

All About Shogunyan

Tribe: Brave/Legendary
Ability: Mad samurai-sword skills
Backstory: He's Jibanyan's Yo-kai ancestor.
Signature Style: Always has a samurai sword at his waist
Loves: Cake—the ancient version of chocobars

Robonyan may very well be the only Yo-kai robot in existence. His origin and backstory are unclear. But he claims to be a robotic version of Jibanyan from the future. According to Robonyan, Jibanyan must one day make a choice: Either stay as he is, or turn into a robot in order to save his friends. Jibanyan doesn't like the idea of becoming a robot. But at least having a chocobar factory installed inside your belly doesn't sound so bad . . .

All About Robonyan

Tribe: Tough

Ability: He is the ultimate robot Yo-kai.

Back-to-the-Future Story: He's a robotic version of Jibanyan from the future.

Secret: He has a built-in chocobar factory.

Mission: Unknown

This go-with-the-flow Yo-kai is a kappa—a harmless creature usually found in lakes, rivers, and streams. As far as Yo-kai go, Walkappa doesn't do too much. The biggest influence he has on people is to make them want to relax.

Kappas usually stick to the water because if their head plates go dry, they lose their powers. But Walkappa has figured out a way around this problem: He keeps a water bottle on hand, and every so often he empties it on top of his head as he walks around.

Nate heard rumors of something strange happening down by the creek. People said a weird looking "duck dude" with a dish on his head was spotted in the water.

All About Walkappa

Tribe: Charming
Ability: Makes people chill out
Looks Like: A duck-dude with a plate on his head
Favorite Food: Enjoys pizza, man
Catchphrase: "Totally bogus, man."

Nate went to investigate, and lo and behold, that's where he met Walkappa. The Yo-kai was happy to introduce himself. But Whisper mistook an actual dish floating in the creek for the kappa. *Awkward.*

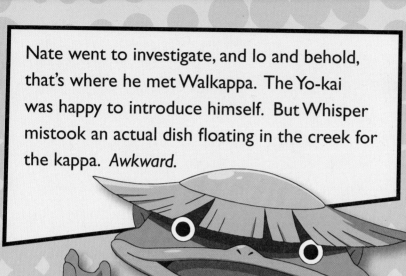

Walkappa

Jeepers creepers, this spooky little Yo-kai makes sure *no one* is a secret keeper. Tattletell looks like a harmless grandmother, but don't be fooled. She clings upside down to her victims' chins and forces them to spill all their deepest secrets.

Nate was minding his own business when out of the blue, Katie told the whole school that he'd done something stinky in the boys' bathroom. Why would Katie embarrass him like that?! Whisper insisted a Yo-kai must be to blame, and Nate used the Yo-kai Watch to reveal Tattletell hanging from Katie's chin.

All About Tattletell

Tribe: Mysterious

Ability: Forces people to reveal their innermost secrets

Worst Secret Spilled: Let's just say it involved a trip to the bathroom.

Enjoys: A good cup of tea and a chat

Catchphrase: "Tattle-tellllllllll!"

Nate quickly summoned Walkappa to deal with the tiny Yo-kai. Try as she might, Tattletell couldn't get Walkappa to spill any secrets . . . because he doesn't have any! Rather than knocking the secrets out of him, Tattletell found the wind knocked out of her.

While most Yo-kai are common, others are quite rare—like the elusive Noko. This mythological being has the body of a snake and brings whoever he possesses good luck. He can also jump incredibly high, multiply incredibly fast, and disappear into thin air. If you're lucky enough to spot one, you're in for a treat . . . literally!

When Nate's mom brought him a popular whoopee pie from Banter Bakery, Nate had a feeling something was up. Those scrumptious treats had a waiting list a mile long—there was no way his mom just happened to score one without the help of a Yo-kai! The tasty treat was indeed the work of Noko. Though Noko disappeared before Whisper could see him (and Whisper was adamant that he hadn't been there at all), Nate sure was glad the little Yo-kai had popped by to visit.

All About Noko

Tribe: Slippery

Ability: Brings people good luck

Backstory: He's the Yo-kai of legends.

Unique Trait: Constantly blushes.
What a cutie!

Catchphrase: "Noko, noko!"

NOKO

Manjimutt used to be an average human businessman. But after losing his job, he roamed the streets—until the day a pile of wood accidentally hit him and a toy poodle at the same time. Thus, Manjimutt was born!

Manjimutt has the ability to make people share his misery. In reality, all he has to do is share his backstory to make people feel sorry for him. But don't feel *too* sorry for him. This downtrodden dog is going to make it big one day—just you wait and see!

Reports of HFD (Human-Faced Dog) sightings were spreading through Springdale. After Katie was totally spooked by her own encounter of the Manjimutt kind, Nate decided he had to stop the shenanigans.

All About Manjimutt

Tribe: Eerie
Ability: Makes people share his misery
What Is He?: Man + Toy Poodle x Wood =
MANJIMUTT
Favorite Drink: Toilet water
Dreams of: Becoming a CEO

As it turned out, Manjimutt just needed someone to listen to his sob story. Now he and Nate are best buds. At least, when Manjimutt isn't landing in jail for loitering or doing his doggy doo-doo in public . . .

Manjimutt's Top Five Career Callings

Pottery

In this dog-eat-dog world, who do you call? Manjimutt will stand up to them all!

Fashion Photographer

Movie Star

Pastry Chef

Hair Stylist

Roughraff

This trash-talking Yo-kai is public enemy number one. He possesses average middle school students, making good kids go bad. We're talking about sassiness, no-good shenanigans, and reckless tomfoolery—things adults look back on and regret. Roughraff loves turning teacher's pets bad-to-the-bone.

Roughraff's rebel-rousing days were numbered when he set his sights on Nate's friend Eddie. First Nate called upon Jibanyan, but Roughraff inspirited the poor kitty. This was clearly a job for a grown-up, and Manjimutt taught Roughraff some manners. In the end, they parted ways with mutual respect.

All About Roughraff

Tribe: Tough

Ability: Turns good kids bad

Responsible for: 98 percent of the troublemakers worldwide

Signature Style: Even his hair is trouble!

Catchphrase: "Rats!"

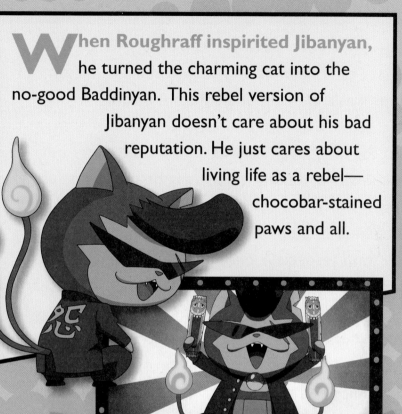

When Roughraff inspirited Jibanyan, he turned the charming cat into the no-good Baddinyan. This rebel version of Jibanyan doesn't care about his bad reputation. He just cares about living life as a rebel—chocobar-stained paws and all.

All About Baddinyan

Tribe: Charming

Ability: Eating chocobars right before dinner

Known for: Not throwing away the wrappers, and not caring a cat's tail about it!

Secretly Wants: To be Next HarMEOWny's bodyguard

Catchphrase: "It's good to be bad."

Hungramps is so gentle, he wouldn't hurt a fly. He just can't help making people hungry. In life, Hungramps was a caring grandfather who took his granddaughter to a special convenience store whenever they were together. Even now as a Yo-kai, he hangs out by that same store, waiting for the day he might see his granddaughter just one more time.

Nate needed to stop Hungramps from making people eat greasy food (especially once Katie became inspirited). So he summoned Tattletell to persuade the Yo-kai to share his story. The old Yo-kai admitted he didn't remember what his granddaughter looked like, and agreed to go on his way. But as luck would have it, a young woman holding the same bear Hungramps had given his granddaughter walked by, and his memory came flooding back.

All About Hungramps

Tribe: Heartful

Ability: Makes people hungry

Secret: He can't remember what his granddaughter looks like.

Best Yo-kai Friend: Tattletell

Catchphrase: "I'm hungry."

Nate was glad to reunite the grandfather and granddaughter—at least Hungramps could see her again.

57

What's a hat to do when its owner tosses it away without so much as a "see you soon"? Turn into a memory-eating Yo-kai, of course! Wazzat used to be a hat, but he became bitter when his owner decided he wasn't fashionable and forgot all about him. Now he spends his days munching on people's memories. It can be good if there's an embarrassing moment you'd rather not remember. But it can be bad when he makes you forget to dress for school.

At first, Nate wasn't sure what to make of Wazzat. The memory-munching Yo-kai helped Katie forget an awkward thing Nate had said about her. Next, Wazzat made the teacher forget about the big test. It seemed too good to be true ...

And it was. Wazzat turned on Nate and tried to erase his memory permanently.

All About Wazzat

Tribe: Mysterious

Ability: Makes people forget things

Backstory: Used to be a normal hat. Now he's a hat Yo-kai who's seriously flipped his lid.

Secret: Just doesn't want to be forgotten

Catchphrase: "Ignorance is bliss."

Manjimutt came to the rescue, knowing his memories would be too foul for even Wazzat to stomach. Nate and the spooky hat agreed to be friends, and Nate promised never to forget him ... unless Wazzat made him.

Illoo is a powerful illusionist who casts hallucinations on those he inspirits. Coupled with the fact that he has the heart of a prankster, and you have some serious Yo-kai mischief on your hands.

Illoo's illusions can seem good at first, like an all-you-can-eat buffet appearing when you're starving. But once the illusion fades, and you realize you've been munching on your own coat sleeve, you'll be disillusioned.

Nate was surprised when girls asked his friends Bear and Eddie out on Valentine's Day. But when the girls asked out *every* boy in school *except* him, he knew something had to be going down. (He wasn't *that* unlovable, was he?)

All About Illoo
Tribe: Mysterious
Ability: Causes hallucinations
Known for: Being a master of illusion
Catchphrase: "Hoo, hoo, hoo!"

Sure enough, Illoo was up to his old tricks. Nate kicked a soccer ball right through the illusion and gained his medal. The first thing he asked for? An illusion of his secret crush, Katie, asking *him* out. Hey, a boy can dream, right?

Blazion is a feisty little fellow. This pumped-up Yo-kai inspirits people to feel super motivated and extra competitive. "Hearts on fire" is an understatement when it comes to Blazion's power. He'll have you cleaning your room, doing your homework, and running a marathon—all before breakfast. Blazion doesn't believe in breaks. Go for the gold and push it to the limit, or pass out trying.

One fateful student service day in Springdale, Blazion was watching from the shadows. He decided it was GO time for Nate and his friends. The next thing Nate knew, he'd volunteered his team to sweep the park walkways, pick up the trash, and even scrub the toilets. Luckily, Happierre made the fiery Yo-kai cool off long enough for Nate and his friends to catch their breaths.

All About Blazion

Tribe: Brave
Ability: Makes people feel competitive
Unique Trait: He has fire burning in his heart... and eyes... and hair.
Secret: He's a martial arts expert.
Mantra: Freeloaders and slackers get nowhere in life.

The park may have been spotless, but everyone deserves a break!

This moody bugster sure is a buzz kill. Negatibuzz makes people feel sad and filled with self-doubt. His influence can have pretty devastating effects. It's one thing if an ice cream vendor doesn't feel up to serving banana splits. It's another when a neurosurgeon goes into an operating room and suddenly questions his purpose in life.

It was a bad day for Nate when he had a toothache and his dentist didn't have the courage to treat the cavity. Luckily, Whisper was able to spot the culprit. Negatibuzz was hovering nearby, sapping all the confidence out of Dr. Smiles.

All About Negatibuzz

Tribe: Shady

Ability: Fills people with doubt

Known for: Bringing people down at the worst possible time

Looks Like: A grumpy mosquito in a hoodie

Catchphrase: "If that's okay."

Desperate to make his tooth better, Nate summoned Blazion, and the fiery Yo-kai whipped Dr. Smiles back into shape before you could say "open wide." Meanwhile, Negatibuzz floated away to sulk in a corner somewhere appropriately shady.

et ready for a shock,
because Signibble's
about to zap it to you!
This mischievous Yo-kai is
surging with energy and
can manipulate electricity.
Whenever someone's cell phone
battery dies, or their television
channel mysteriously changes, or they can't
get a Wi-Fi signal, it's likely because Signibble is
munching on
their power
supply.

All About Signibble

Tribe: Mysterious

Ability: Manipulating electricity

Soultimate Move: Signal Shock

Likes: Causing mischief

Catchphrase: "Zap, zap!"

Signibble

Nate and his friends were having a sleepover and sneakily tuned in to some late-night television. But Signibble had other plans. He changed the channel whenever the programming got good. Unfortunately, Jibanyan wanted to watch, too, and Signibble's interference made him very *nyangry*. The furious kitty battled Signibble with a vacuum cleaner, but he just wound up waking up Nate's parents and getting everyone in trouble.

Oh my swirls, what's a sweet country Yo-kai to do when he gets lost in the hustle and bustle of the big city? Eat other people's ice cream, of course! Komasan is an innocent country bumpkin who just can't rightly control himself when he catches a whiff of that sweet, sugary stuff. He's learned to time it just right so he can sneak a lick of other people's ice cream when they're not looking.

Komasan was fixin' to wait for his brother in the Japanese gardens when a festival showed up. And what did Komasan see? People eating all sorts of ice cream! Once Komasan got a taste of those heavenly swirls, he knew he needed more. So he packed up and headed to the big city, where the buildings are tall and the ice cream flows like a river in springtime. Nate tried to show the sweet little guy around, but Komasan quickly realized the city might be just *too* big for a wide-eyed country boy like himself.

All About Komasan

Tribe: Charming
Ability: Steals a lick of people's ice cream
Speaks with: A country accent
Likes: Writing home to Mama
Catchphrase: "Oh my swirls!"

Komasan

This starry-eyed tyke is Komasan's little brother, and he looks up to his big bro more than anyone in the whole wide Yo-kai world. Unlike other Yo-kai, Komajiro doesn't rightly inspirit people. He's just fixin' to learn all there is to know about life in the city. He may be scared, but as long as his big brother is around, Komajiro knows that everything will be right as rain.

Just when it looked like Komasan was ready to pack up his rucksack and hop the next train back to the country,

All About Komajiro

Tribe: Charming

Ability: Why, he wouldn't inspirit a person any more than snow would fall in summertime!

Mission: To learn all there is to know about life in the big city.

Personal Hero: Komasan, of course

Catchphrase: "Oh, big brother, lookie here!"

his little brother, Komajiro, showed up.

Now that they're back together, Komajiro is pleased as punch! He can't wait for Komasan to show him what he's learned about life in the big city. Looks like these little fellas still have a lot of adventure left before headin' home to Mama.

Meet Uh-Uh-Uh, No-Siree-Bob, and That's-Not-It —otherwise known as the Nosirs. This Yo-kai trio spreads doubt and insecurity, making people question their decisions. It's bad enough when you're lost and can't decide if you should go left or right, or when you're taking a test and you second-guess every answer you fill in.

All About the Nosirs

Tribe: Eerie

Ability: Make people question their decisions.

Signature Style: Preppy sweater vests

Secret: They just want to feel useful.

Not-So-Secret Secret: That's-Not-It suffers from nasal congestion.

But even worse is that one of the Nosirs has a giant booger hanging out of his nose. That's just gross.

It was the day of the big test in Nate's class, but none of his classmates could decide on the answers! Nate knew a Yo-kai must be to blame, and that's when he discovered the Nosirs. They almost had Nate and Whisper under their spell of self-doubt. But when Nate thanked them for making him second-guess the way he'd put a Yo-kai Medal in his watch (he'd put it in upside down), the Nosirs had a change of heart. Uh-Uh-Uh even inspirited Nate's Yo-kai Watch so he could always be useful. What a weird day!

Some Yo-kai can be truly troublesome. Take Fidgephant, a Yo-kai who uses his powers to make you have to go to the bathroom at the worst possible time, such as during a movie or a test. Fidgephant isn't being mean, he's just acting out because he himself is under tremendous pressure. But still, that's no reason to make everyone suffer along with you!

Nate couldn't believe every boy in school had to hit the restroom at the exact same time unless a Yo-kai was up to its tricks. Sure enough, Fidgephant was roaming the school, putting pressure on all the students. Nate summoned Wazzat to help. The hat munched on Fidgephant's memories and discovered the Yo-kai himself felt weighed down by life's pressures. All it took was a little mind-numbing relief from Wazzat to get Fidgephant to let it go.

All About Fidgephant

Tribe: Tough

Ability: Makes people have to go, as in answer the call of nature or see a man about a horse.

Likes: Waterfalls

Known for: Being a toughie

Catchphrase: "So much pressure—let it out!"

Fidgephant

This poor little Yo-kai can't help hiding in the dark—he's afraid of his own shadow. But he doesn't like being alone, so he inspirits people to lock themselves away from the rest of the world along with him. He can be a pretty tricky Yo-kai to catch. After all, he's had a lifetime of practice hiding. But if you have a dark closet or locked chest in your room, it might as well have a flashing WELCOME sign for the likes of Hidabat.

All About Hidabat

Tribe: Shady

Ability: Makes people lock themselves away

Can Be Found in: Caves, closets, under beds

Not-So-Secret Secret: Everything frightens him.

Trademark: Emits ultrasonic waves that only Yo-kai can hear

When Jibanyan locked himself in Nate's room and swore he would never come out, it was big trouble for Nate. All his stuff was in there! Luckily, Whisper picked up on Hidabat's ultrasonic waves and alerted Nate that a Yo-kai was afoot.

Happierre convinced Jibanyan to leave the room, and Fidgephant shocked the little bat right out of the cat with urgency of the number-one kind. But when Hidabat confessed how scared he was, Nate couldn't help feeling sorry for him. Nate offered to let him live in his closet, and just like that, Nate's Yo-kai boardinghouse gained another supernatural tenant.

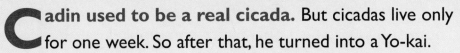

Cadin used to be a real cicada. But cicadas live only for one week. So after that, he turned into a Yo-kai. This buggy Yo-kai doesn't actually want to bug anyone at all. He'd just rather sleep underground and mind his own business. He can set off buried treasure detectors. But as far as Yo-kai go, this little guy is pretty harmless.

All About Cadin

Tribe: Charming

Ability: Sets off buried treasure detectors

Signature Style: Carries a samurai sword. Why? It's not important.

Heart's Desire: Just wants to play and have fun

Catchphrase: "Ming Ming!"

Nate and Whisper accidentally discovered Cadin buried underground when Nate was helping his friends dig for treasure. And the little Yo-kai was *not* happy to be found. Since he lived for only one week as a real cicada, Cadin thought he had only one week to live as a Yo-kai unless he stayed underground. But once the clock started ticking, Cadin just wanted to play and have fun with what time he had left. So that's what they did. And as luck would have it, Cadin's time wasn't up at the end of the week. He just fell asleep!

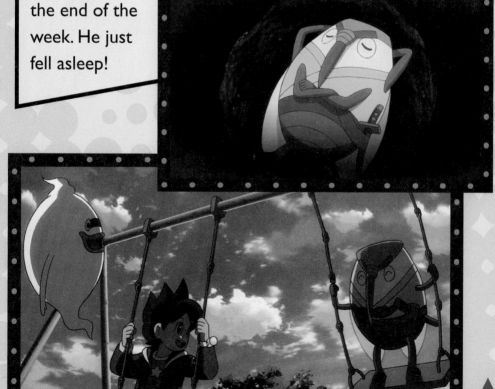

Poor Buhu. She tries not to be a nuisance—she really does. But it's in her Yo-kai nature to bring bad luck and disappointment wherever she goes. This sad-looking bird gives people a false feeling of good fortune before crushing their dreams at the last second. You have to feel for her. It can't be pleasant being the embodiment of bad luck and disappointment wherever you go. *Boo-hoo.*

All About Buhu

Tribe: Eerie
Ability: Brings people bad luck
Secretly Wants: To catch the eye of an attractive bird
Unique Trait: She's one sad-looking fowl.
Catchphrase: "Boo, hoo, hoo!"

I try not to be a nuisance.

Nate was super stoked to think he was getting the last doughnut at Banter Bakery. Too bad Buhu dashed his hopes—the bakery ran out of doughnuts just as Nate reached the counter! Buhu didn't stop there. She made Bear think he'd aced a test before the teacher said he'd lost a point for not writing his name. That was enough for Nate, and he summoned Robonyan to right Buhu's wrongs. Robonyan added Bear's name to the test in artificially aged ink so he got his perfect score after all. And Buhu was glad to finally not be the nuisance she always is . . . if only for a moment.

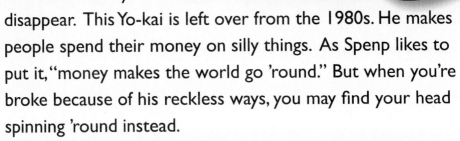

Hold tight to your wallet, because when Spenp is around, there's no telling how he'll make your allowance disappear. This Yo-kai is left over from the 1980s. He makes people spend their money on silly things. As Spenp likes to put it, "money makes the world go 'round." But when you're broke because of his reckless ways, you may find your head spinning 'round instead.

Nate, Eddie, and Bear couldn't wait to purchase the new video game *YOLO Watch 2*. But they spent their money on a giant fish and totem pole instead, and Nate discovered Spenp was to blame. The Yo-kai was thrilled, but the boys were crushed they couldn't afford their video game. Luckily, their purchases qualified them for the mall's raffle, and they won third prize: a copy of *YOLO Watch 2*!

All About Spenp

Tribe: Slippery

Ability: Makes people spend all their money on silly stuff

Backstory: He's a change purse from the yuppie era of the 1980s.

Likes: Shopping sprees

Catchphrase: "I work hard and I play hard."

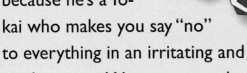

There's no way Noway is letting you say "yes" to things you want to do. That's because he's a Yo-kai who makes you say "no" to everything in an irritating and insulting way. Want to go to that sweet party this weekend? "No way." Want to have the last piece of cake? "No way." Want to stop saying "no way" to everything? You get the drift.

When Katie invited Nate to her weekend barbecue, the only thing he wanted to say was "yes." But thanks to

All About Noway

Tribe: Tough

Ability: Makes people say "no way" to everything

Secret: Just wants a friend, but everyone keeps saying "no way."

Looks Like: A wall

Catchphrase: "No Way" (obviously)

Noway's interference, he said "no way" instead. Nate and Whisper confronted Noway on the school roof, and Nate quickly realized the only way to beat someone who says "no" all the time is to ask the opposite. As soon as Nate asked Noway not to be his friend, the troublesome Yo-kai handed over his medal.

As far as Yo-kai go, Cheeksqueek really stinks! He makes people fart uncontrollably at the worst possible times—just for the fun of it. Sure, it can't be easy when your face looks like a butt . . . literally. But Cheeksqueek seems quite proud of his tootie-bootie ways. As Whisper puts it, this guy is Just. The. Worst.

It was bad enough that Cheeksqueek made Katie stink up the classroom with embarrassing toots. But when the fiendish little Yo-kai made Nate fart so badly he cleared the whole school, it was vengeance time.

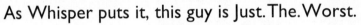

All About Cheeksqueek

Tribe: Eerie

Ability: Makes people toot

Responsible for: The Great Flatulence Pandemic of 2007

Looks Like: A giant tush

Catchphrase: "Poo-poo!"

This battle called for a Yo-kai who wouldn't have foul-smelling farts. So Nate summoned Robonyan to the rescue. (Because robots from the future can alter the scent of their own toots. Bet you didn't know that!) By forcing Cheeksqueek to eat high-gas-content food (i.e., sweet potatoes), Robonyan made Cheeksqueek understand how embarrassing it can be to fart uncontrollably.

Yo-kai **Chatalie** has a big head and an even bigger mouth. Anyone inspirited by her brags shamelessly, shouting promises they can't keep, goals they can't reach, and challenges they'll probably regret. Chatalie uses her

pink cell phone to inspirit people as far as the signal will reach. She's pretty proud of her big-talk ways. In fact, she'll never let you hear the end of it.

All About Chatalie

Tribe: Eerie

Ability: Makes people brag

Secret Weapon: Her inspiriting pink cell phone

Known for: Being *that* loud talker on the bus or train

Catchphrase: "If you've got it, flaunt it."

When Chatalie came to Springdale, she set her sights on Bear. She made him brag about perfect test scores and running records. Even though everyone knows Bear can be full of hot air, Nate could tell this was above and beyond his usual bodacious bragging. Nate used the Yo-kai Watch to reveal Chatalie, and after some tough talk from Blazion, the chatty chatterbox changed her tune. But not before leaving a parting gift: She inspirited Eddie to make crazy student council promises—and convinced him to run for president of the United States.

When the beat don't stop, you've gotta dance till you drop! So say Wiglin, Steppa, and Rhyth. These movin' and groovin' Yo-kai keep the dance party rocking all day and night . . . whether you want to or not. They inspirit people to boogie anytime, anywhere. When is enough enough? Let's just say that this trio has been dancing for centuries and shows no signs of stopping.

It was pretty sweet when these three hip Yo-kai helped Nate show off some killer dance moves during gym class. It was less sweet when they made him show off those same moves during math class.

All About Wiglin, Steppa, and Rhyth

Tribe: Heartful
Ability: They make people dance . . . a LOT.
Look Like: Wiggly pieces of seaweed
Secret: You can't stop the beat when it's in your soul.
Catchphrase: "Dance like no one's watching!"

Nate tried to reason with them, but they were too busy bopping to the beat to listen. Nate better break out his dance shoes, because his life just got a whole lot more groovin'.

Call the fashion police: Dazzabel is breaking all the rules. This dolled-up Yo-kai inspirits people to dress in bizarre clothes and parade their outlandish styles all over town. We're talking acid-washed overalls. Sequined rompers. And BOWS. Fashions may come and go, but for Dazzabel, crazy never goes out of style.

It was full-on crisis mode when Dazzabel made Nate's mom head to his parent-teacher conference dressed like a Mardi Gras parade float. (And not the good kind.) Nate summoned the dowdiest Yo-kai he knew—Hungramps—to talk some fashion sense into Dazzabel. Too bad for Nate, Dazzabel just made Hungramps look cool with a funky, new surfer outfit. She even whipped up a tux and bow tie for Whisper! Was Nate going to have to change schools to escape the embarrassment of his mother's temporary fashion insanity?

All About Dazzabel

Tribe: Charming

Ability: Makes people dress in ridiculous outfits

Responsible for: Fashion faux pas around the world

Loves: BOWS

Catchphrase: "Faaaaaancy!"

Dazzabel

It's okay. **Don't mind Dimmy.** He's just going to make you blend into the background, if it's okay with you. This Shady Yo-kai doesn't want to be a bother, but he can't seem to stop inspiriting people. Dimmy makes those he possesses become a dim shadow of their former selves. But it's okay, don't worry. Nothing really matters, anyway.

All About Dimmy

Tribe: Shady
Ability: Makes people a shadow of their former selves
Not-So-Secret Secret: Just wants to blend in
Known for: He's great at hide-and-seek.
Catchphrase: "It's okay, don't worry about me."

94

Just when Nate's mother was about to reach the school in Dazzabel's outlandish attire, Nate and Whisper managed to summon Dimmy. Surely the "I just want to blend in" Yo-kai could talk some sense into Dazzabel. But Nate quickly became inspirited, and it was up to Whisper to set things right. With a quick nudge (read: shove) in the right direction, Dimmy collided with Dazzabel, and their powers canceled each other out. Dazzabel was de-dazzled. Nate's mom ran home in embarrassment. And Nate . . . well, Nate was still inspirited by Dimmy. So he just wanted to stay out of the way.

It's fairly common to get dazed when the bathwater is too hot, but who knew such a pigheaded bully was to blame? Sproink is the Yo-kai who makes people feel light-headed when the water is too warm. According to Sproink, the bath isn't hot enough unless you feel like passing out. According to everyone else, Sproink can enjoy the hot bath alone.

Nate and his friends were just chilling at the public hot springs when the water temperature went from super-relaxing to super-scalding. Sproink had taken over the pool, and he wouldn't leave unless Nate made him.

Blazion and Roughraff tried to teach Sproink a lesson, but they both ended up in hot water. At the end of the day, it took an old man who liked the water at volcanic temperatures to best the hotheaded Yo-kai, who couldn't take the heat.

All About Sproink

Ability: **Makes people dizzy when the bathwater is too warm**

Personality: **Stubborn. Super stubborn.**

Can Be Found in: **Hot tubs and public baths**

Catchphrase: **"You guys are wimps."**

Sproink

Didja hear the story about the Yo-kai who makes people talk on and on? He's one heck of a storyteller, you know, you KNOW. And so it goes with Babblong, the most annoying Yo-kai you'll ever meet. This spirit makes people tell long, rambling stories that go on forever. His power has been on the rise recently because of the Internet. In a world where everyone loves to over share, a blabber like Babblong is king!

It was a cruel day at Springdale Elementary when Mr. Johnson wouldn't stop talking, even after the bell rang. But add to that a rambling encounter with Katie in the hall, and Nate knew Babblong was lurking. He tried to summon Wazzat to deal with the talkative spirit.

All About Babblong

Tribe: Slippery

Ability: Makes people talk uncontrollably

Known for: Stories about his Uncle Lester. He literally can't stop talking about him.

Unique Trait: Enormous nose

Catchphrase: "You know? You KNOW?"

But Babblong inspirited Nate before he could use his medal. With some quick thinking on Jibanyan's part, Wazzat appeared and erased Babblong's stories. When you have a running mouth but nothing to say, your story will run out of steam before it begins.

There's only one word in Peppillon's dictionary: EXCITED! This colorful butterfly makes people overly enthusiastic about ordinary stuff. In fact, Peppillon is the Yo-kai responsible for making parents drag their kids to boring places and events like museums or history reenactments. It's true that the things Peppillon pumps you up about may not be that interesting. But it's also true the world would be a much more boring place without him.

Nate couldn't understand why his parents were so excited about taking him to see some boring waterfall for spring break. But once he realized Peppillon was

All About Peppillon

Tribe: Heartful
Ability: Makes people feel overexcited about boring stuff
Likes: Sunshine, rainbows
Hates: Rain
Catchphrase: "Let's go!"

inspiriting them, it all made sense. Whisper convinced Nate to let the butterfly Yo-kai stick around—after all, the trip was already planned, and spring break would be a real downer without him. And as it turned out, Nate and his family had a pretty great time. Could anything rain on their parade?

Drizzle's name says it all. This is the Yo-kai who makes it rain, as in sprinkle, pour cats and dogs, and rain on your wedding day. He's not really out to cause mischief. Rain is just kind of his thing. It's like there's a dark cloud constantly following him. No, wait . . . there's *literally* a dark cloud constantly following him. At least there's no guessing game when it comes to his powers.

Yes, yes, something would rain on Nate's spring break parade. Just as his family was watching the waterfall, Drizzle showed up and

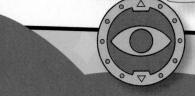

All About Drizzle

Tribe: Eerie

Ability: Makin' it rain

Heart's Desire: He wouldn't mind a nice, thick towel.

Forecast: 100 percent chance of showers. Forever.

Secret: You can't make a rainbow without him.

made it pour. Peppillon flew away, Nate's parents realized a waterfall is just a waterfall, and they all ran for cover.

Longing for sunshine, Nate summoned Robonyan to scare the Eerie downpour-er away. Once the rain stopped, a rainbow appeared, ending Nate's spring break on a cheery note after all.

Mirapo

If you've ever closed your eyes while riding in the backseat of a car only to open them and find you've reached your destination, then you probably have Mirapo to thank. This oversized mirror creates wormholes that allow people to travel instantaneously to their destinations. He got Nate's family back home lickety-split after their spring break excursion. Not a bad Yo-kai to have around when you're stuck in traffic.

All About Mirapo

Tribe: Mysterious

Ability: Transports people to their destinations while they sleep

Responsible for: When you wake up in your own bed but don't remember how you got there

Attracted to: Shiny things

Enjoys: Reflecting on his memories

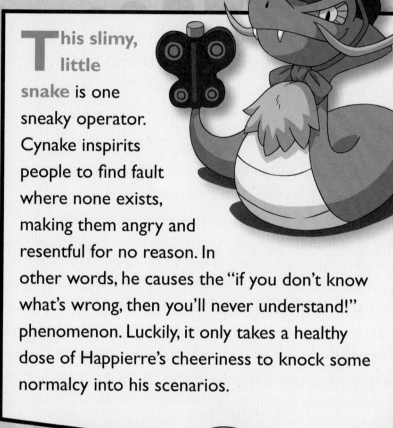

T his slimy, little snake is one sneaky operator. Cynake inspirits people to find fault where none exists, making them angry and resentful for no reason. In other words, he causes the "if you don't know what's wrong, then you'll never understand!" phenomenon. Luckily, it only takes a healthy dose of Happierre's cheeriness to knock some normalcy into his scenarios.

All About Cynake

Tribe: Slippery
Ability: Makes people find fault where there isn't any
Enjoys: A good argument over nothing
Secret: He just wants attention.
Catchphrase: "Humph!"

Always leave them ... *not* wanting more? Rockabelly's got it going on when it comes to worn-out fads. He's responsible for the rise and fall of a very creepy belly-dancing phenomenon: drawing a weird-looking face on your stomach and then making it *dance*. Like all fads, Rockabelly's was funny at first. Then his shenanigans got old. Now having him around is just awkward.

It was weird when Eddie began showing off the latest fad sweeping Springdale: belly dancing with a face painted on his stomach. But when Mr. Johnson joined in the bizarre fun, it was clearly time to break out the Yo-kai Watch.

Nate revealed Rockabelly and called upon Dismarelda to stop the inappropriate belly-wiggling before Rockabelly could put Katie under her spell, too.

All About Rockabelly

Tribe: Eerie

Ability: Causes people to draw a creepy face on their stomach and make it dance

Responsible for: The "this is getting really annoying" phenomenon

Looks Like: A chicken. With a face on its belly.

Catchphrase: "Ready?"

Nate's plan worked . . . until Rockabelly inspirited him instead. Well, at least he managed to keep one stomach in the classroom covered—even if it wasn't his own.

Rockabelly

Other Characters

Mr. Aaron Adams

Mr. Adams is Nate's father. He works hard, is always optimistic, and is a generally upbeat person. Unless a dismal Yo-kai crosses his path. Then it's up to Nate to set things right!

Mrs. Lily Adams

Nate's mom is practical and disciplined, which can be tough for Nate since he doesn't like cleaning his room! She is constantly making sure Nate does his homework, finishes his chores, and isn't getting into mischief. If only the Yo-kai wouldn't keep Nate from doing all of the above . . .

Mr. Jason Forester

Katie's father is a skilled businessman who's highly respected by his coworkers. Though he works hard, he always makes time for his daughter and wife.

Mrs. Rebecca Forester

Katie's mother is a lot like her daughter: gentle and caring, and also confident and driven. Once Katie worried her mom would be furious about a bad grade she got on a test. But Katie's mom understood and encouraged her to do better next time.

Mr. Hank Bernstein

Hank Bernstein manages a supply store in Springdale. Bear looks up to his dad and gets his gruff personality from him. But both Bear and his dad know who's really in charge of their family . . . Bear's mom.

Other Characters

Mrs. Barbara Bernstein

Barbara Bernstein loves her son more than anything in the world . . . and don't you forget it! She can be scary when anybody messes with her little Barnaby, whom she calls "pookie-bear."

Mr. Jim Archer

Eddie's father is a famous architect and loves state-of-the-art technology. He is often away on business trips, but Eddie keeps up the family tradition of tech savvy while he's on the road.

Mrs. Yvette Archer

Yvette Archer is very enthusiastic about her son's education— perhaps a little too enthusiastic about it. She wants him to excel, but has a hard time watching her little boy growing up so quickly. Maybe it's because she sees so much of his dad in him.

Mr. Joe Johnson

Mr. Johnson is Nate's homeroom teacher. He's kindhearted, but he doesn't let anything slide. And Nate can have a hard time staying out of trouble when there's a Yo-kai on Mr. Johnson's head causing mischief.

Nate is meeting more Yo-kai every day, and they're only getting weirder. Who knows what adventures lie in store for him and his Yo-kai friends?

Whatever happens from here on out, I can promise you one thing: Your life is never going to be the same!